PUPPY PATROL ™

LITTLE STAR

JENNY DALE

Illustrations by Mick Reid
Cover illustration by Michael Rowe

AN
APPLE
PAPERBACK

SCHOLASTIC INC.
New York Toronto London Auckland Sydney
Mexico City New Delhi Hong Kong Buenos Aires

SPECIAL THANKS TO CHERITH BALDRY

No part of this publication may be reproduced, in whole or in part, or stored in a retrieval system, or transmitted in any form or by any means, electronic, mechanical, photocopying, recording, or otherwise, without the written permission of the publisher. For information regarding permission, please write to Macmillan Publishers Ltd., 20 New Wharf Rd., London N1 9RR Basingstoke and Oxford.

ISBN 0-439-54363-0

Copyright © 2001 by Working Partners Limited.
Illustrations copyright © 2001 by Mick Reid.

All rights reserved. Published by Scholastic Inc., 557 Broadway, New York, NY 10012, by arrangement with Macmillan Children's Books, a division of Macmillan Publishers Ltd.

SCHOLASTIC and associated logos are trademarks and/or registered trademarks of Scholastic Inc.

12 11 10 9 8 7 6 5 4 3 2 1   3 4 5 6 7 8/0

Printed in the U.S.A.
First Scholastic printing, October 2003

CHAPTER ONE

"**C**ome on, Em!" Neil Parker stopped outside the door of Meadowbank School and waited impatiently for his sister. "I want to get home and walk Jake before it gets dark."

Neil's breath billowed out in a cloud in the frosty air. A thin dusting of snow covered the playground, and the gray sky threatened more snow to come. Neil pulled his cap down over his spiky brown hair and stamped his feet to keep warm. "Come *on!*" he repeated.

Emily, Neil's ten-year-old sister, was struggling with a rolled-up poster, her bulging schoolbag, and a papier-mâché donkey she'd made for her class's Christmas manger. "I'm coming," she said. "I've got tons of things to take home." A huge smile spread across her face. "I can't wait for Christmas!"

"I know." Neil grinned in return. "And no more school for three whole weeks. Just dogs all day, every day!"

Neil and Emily's parents, Bob and Carole Parker, ran King Street Kennels and Rescue Center, just outside the little country town of Compton. Neil and his family loved dogs so much that Neil's friends called them the Puppy Patrol.

As he and Emily hurried down the side of the school toward the bike sheds, Neil thought about Jake, his young Border collie. He imagined days and days playing together in the exercise field behind the house, or out in the park. Not to mention lots of training sessions in the barn.

Just as they approached the corner by the garbage cans, they heard a dog begin to bark. A small child started to wail loudly.

"Oh, no! I wonder what's going on?" said Emily.

Neil frowned. "I don't recognize that bark. It's definitely not Dotty." Dotty was the excitable Dalmatian owned by Mr. Hamley, the school principal.

Neil and Emily ran even faster. As they turned the corner, they saw a small boy from the preschool class. He was howling with his eyes shut tight and the contents of his bag scattered at his feet.

Julie Baker, from Emily's class, was kneeling down beside the little boy. She was trying to comfort him while Neil's good friend Chris Wilson peered nervously at something behind the garbage cans.

The barking had turned into a low growling noise, but Neil couldn't see what was making it. "What is it?" he asked.

"It's a strange dog," Julie said. She sounded scared. "Come and look, Neil."

As Neil went over to the garbage cans, one of them crashed over, spilling trash out onto the playground. A big dog appeared from behind the can, pushed his head into the trash, and started rooting hungrily through the discarded food wrappers.

The dog had a smooth black coat with tan markings around his face and on his paws. His ears were pointed and he had a short, stumpy tail. *A Doberman*, thought Neil. He knew they could be aggressive if they weren't handled properly.

"What happened?" Emily asked. She dumped her things on the ground and went to help Julie look after the little boy.

"The dog was just hanging around," Chris explained. "Mark went up to pet him, and the dog snarled at him and grabbed his bag."

"Did he bite him?" Emily asked anxiously. She gave the little boy a gentle smile. "Mark, did the dog hurt you?"

Mark shook his head. He was starting to calm down. "He took my chocolate," he sobbed, pointing to an empty chocolate bar wrapper.

Emily let out a sigh of relief.

Neil went over to Mark and stood looking down at him. "You should never try to pet a strange dog," he explained kindly. "You probably frightened him."

"Leave it to you, Neil!" Chris exclaimed with a grin. "It's never the dog's fault, is it?"

"There are no problem dogs, only problem owners," Neil said, repeating something his dad always said. "What's this one doing here? That's what I'd like to know."

He turned back to the dog, which had pulled a half-eaten sandwich out of the garbage and was wolfing it down ravenously. Neil realized that he was quite a young dog. His dark coat, which should have been sleek and glossy, looked dull and uncared for, and he was so thin that all his ribs were showing. A heavy studded collar hung loosely around his neck.

"He's been living on the streets for a while," Neil said. "Just look at him!"

The dog finished the sandwich and looked around, flattening his ears and letting out a growl from deep in his throat.

"Neil, move away," Julie said nervously.

"It's OK," Neil reassured her. "The dog won't attack us if we don't bother him."

He looked around to see that several more of his friends had come over and were standing around uncertainly, looking at the strange dog.

"Just walk past quietly," Neil directed them. "He's not dangerous if you don't scare him."

Neil waited until the others had gone, and then carefully took a step toward the dog. At once it lowered its head, and the growling grew louder and more threatening.

"Neil, don't," Emily said. "We need to get Dad."

"OK," Neil agreed. He had to admit that tackling the dog by himself might not be the best idea. "You go — I'll keep an eye on the dog."

Emily collected Mark's scattered belongings and put them back in his bag. Then she took the little boy's hand. "We'll go to the preschoolers' playground and find Mark's mom," she said. "I bet Dad will be there, too, picking up Sarah."

"Don't let Sarah come over here!" Neil called after her. He knew how their five-year-old sister insisted on cuddling all the dogs that came to King Street. This dog didn't look cuddly at all.

Chris and Julie went to the shed to get their bikes while Neil stood watching the dog. It had started pawing through the contents of the garbage can.

He couldn't remember anyone phoning the kennel to ask about a lost Doberman, but he hoped that somewhere a frantic owner was trying to trace their pet. *Thank goodness the dog has an identity tag on his collar*, thought Neil. He was pretty sure the dog could soon be reunited with his owner.

A few minutes later, Bob Parker strode around the corner, dangling a muzzle and leash from one hand. Bob was a big man, with broad shoulders and a bushy brown beard. He wore a green sweatshirt with the King Street Kennels logo on it. "What's going on?" he asked.

"Chris said the dog was just hanging around," Neil told him. "He seems really hungry."

"It looks like he's been homeless for quite a while," Bob said, studying the dog thoughtfully. "Look how thin he is! But he looks pretty well bred." He took a pace or two toward the dog, with one hand held out. Calmly, he said, "Here, boy. Steady. Come here."

The dog had been sniffing an empty yogurt carton but, as Bob spoke, his head whipped up. He snarled, baring strong white teeth. Cautiously, Bob moved closer, but the dog lunged at him, snapping.

"Dad!" Neil exclaimed in alarm.

Bob kept calm, but he stopped moving forward. "OK. OK, boy," he said soothingly. "Neil, just get his attention for a minute, will you? But don't startle him."

Neil nodded, trying to keep as calm as his dad. He clapped his hands together twice and called, "Hey, boy! Here!"

The Doberman's head swung around. At once, Bob Parker stepped forward and grabbed the dog's collar. He let out a furious bark and began to struggle wildly, paws skidding on the ground, while Bob clipped the muzzle into place.

Neil darted forward to help.

"No, Neil — keep back!" Bob warned.

Neil stopped and watched anxiously as the snapping jaws were held safely in the muzzle and the strap was fastened.

"There," Bob said with a sigh of relief. He stood up, keeping a grip on the Doberman's collar as he clipped on the leash.

"Let me see if I can read his ID tag," said Neil. He walked slowly up to the dog and bent down.

Though the dog tried to pull away, Neil managed to get hold of the tag. "There's a phone number," he told his dad. "A Padsham number, I think. And it says his name's Brutus."

"Great," said Bob. He stroked the Doberman's head. "That means we should be able to trace his owner."

"Come on, Brutus," Neil said, straightening up. "Let's try to get you home for Christmas!"

Back at King Street Kennels, Bob took Brutus to the rescue center while Neil tried calling the number on the tag, but there was only the shrill, drawn-out tone that indicated the number was no longer in service.

Neil sighed with disappointment. Reuniting Brutus with his owner wasn't going to be as easy as he had thought.

Replacing the receiver, he went out to the rescue

center, where he found Bob and Emily settling Brutus into his pen. Bob had already asked Emily to put down bowls of food and water. Cautiously, he led Brutus into the pen and unclipped the muzzle. This time Brutus didn't try to attack him. He made straight for the water bowl and took a long drink.

"He'll be fine," Bob said as he came out of the pen and fastened the door. "But do not go into the pen with him until we're sure he's settled down, OK?"

"OK," said Neil. He watched as Brutus wolfed down the food in the bowl and then flopped down with his nose on his paws.

"He's tired out," said Emily. "Poor thing, he must have been wandering around for weeks."

"Did you manage to reach his owner?" Bob asked.

Neil shook his head and explained that the number on the tag was no longer in service.

"I'll call Sergeant Moorhead," Bob said. "And Terri McCall at the SPCA. Somebody might have reported Brutus missing."

He strode out of the rescue center. Neil and Emily stayed watching Brutus for a minute or two more before checking on the other rescue dogs. There were only two others: a perky black mongrel and a young bullterrier who was watching them bright-eyed through the mesh of the pen.

Neil fed them dog treats from the supply he always kept in his pockets. Luckily, both dogs had already been visited by several families who wanted to take them, and Neil was confident they would be in new homes by Christmas. He wondered if Brutus would be so lucky.

Neil and Emily left the rescue center and hurried across to the house. It was growing dark, and the snow was falling more steadily, covering the court-yard with a layer of white.

Inside, the kitchen was warm and filled with tempting smells of dinner. Carole Parker was stand-ing at the stove, stirring something in a pan. As Neil opened the door, Jake, his young Border collie, leaped up from his basket in the corner and bounded over to him, barking delightedly.

"Hi, Jake!" Neil said, bending over to ruffle the dog's ears. "Mom, I haven't had time to walk Jake. Can I take him out now?"

"No, dinner's almost ready," said Carole. "And it's dark outside. Don't worry, I took him out for a run earlier, before it started snowing so heavily."

"Snow for Christmas!" Neil's little sister Sarah was bouncing up and down at the big kitchen table where she was pasting strips of colored paper to-gether to make a chain. "I'm going to show Fudge how to make a snowman."

Neil groaned. Sarah thought that Fudge, her ham-ster, was smart enough to do anything.

"It's way too cold out for Fudge," said Carole. "Let him stay in his nice, warm cage."

"But Fudge *wants* to make a snowman," Sarah protested.

"No, he doesn't, he's only a hamster," said Neil impatiently. He was still feeling worried that he hadn't been able to contact Brutus's owner.

"Mom!" Sarah's voice rose to a wail. "Neil said —"

"Never mind, Sarah," Emily interrupted quickly. "Tomorrow we'll make a snow hamster together. And Fudge can look at it through the window."

Sarah thought about that for a moment and beamed happily.

"What's for dinner?" Neil asked his mom. "I'm as hungry as Brutus!"

"Chili and rice. Wash your hands, you two, and Sarah, clear your things off the table."

Neil was at the sink in the utility room when his dad came out of the office.

Bob was shaking his head. "The police haven't had any reports of a lost Doberman," he said. "Not here or in Padsham. Neither has the SPCA." He went over to the stove, stirred the pot of rice, and unhooked a colander from the wall to drain it. "Maybe we'll have Brutus with us over Christmas after all," he added.

"His owner must be really worried," said Emily, getting knives and forks out of the kitchen drawer.

Neil knew she was right. He glanced down at Jake, who was sitting beside the table with a hopeful look on his face. He knew how bad he would feel if he had to spend Christmas without his beloved dog.

"We know Brutus's owner lives in Padsham," he said. "It can't be that difficult to find him." He finished drying his hands and came to sit down. "I'm going to try," he announced. "I'll get Brutus home for Christmas if it's the last thing I do!"

CHAPTER TWO

Bob brought the pots of food to the table and everyone sat down. Neil took a forkful of the chili that Carole had spooned onto his plate. "I'll take a picture of Brutus and put it on the web site," he decided.

"And tomorrow I'll call Jake Fielding and see if he'll put something in the *Compton News*," Emily added. Jake Fielding was a photographer for the local paper and had covered several King Street stories in the past.

"And I'll make lots of posters!" said Sarah.

"A couple of posters would be a good idea," Bob said. "One in Mike Turner's veterinary clinic and one over at Jill Walker's — the vet in Padsham."

"Great!" said Neil. "And then we can —"

A knock at the kitchen door interrupted him. Carole got up to open it and Jake gave a welcoming bark as Kate and Glen Paget came in, brushing snow off their coats.

Kate was one of the Parkers' full-time kennel assistants, but she wasn't working at the moment because she was expecting a baby. Her blond hair was tucked under a brightly striped hat and she wore a matching sweater.

"Kate!" said Carole. "Come in and sit down. How are you?"

Kate patted the bulge under her sweater. "Huge," she said, smiling. "And pretty tired. I'll be glad when it's all over."

She sank down into the chair Bob brought for her. Her dog, a pretty Westie cross called Willow, waddled across the kitchen and sat down at her feet. Willow was expecting pups, and looked just as big and uncomfortable as her owner.

"Willow will be glad when it's all over, too," said Kate's husband Glen. "We'll have our hands full soon, with a new baby *and* a litter of pups!"

"I'm really glad that you can take Willow," said Kate. "I can't give her the attention she needs right now and Glen is out all day."

"Hey!" Neil exclaimed, jumping up from the table. "What do you mean, take Willow? What's going on that I don't know about?" He hoped nothing was wrong with the lively little dog — or Kate.

"Sit down and finish your dinner," Carole said. She took her own place again, while Bob put the kettle on to make tea for Kate and Glen. "Kate called me this afternoon. I forgot to tell you, what with everything else that's been going on."

"Like Kate says, she can't give Willow the proper care just now," Bob explained. "She has to rest and make sure her baby's all right. So she asked us if we would look after Willow for the next few days."

"And of course we said yes," Carole finished.

"I'll come and see Willow every day," said Kate, "but I know she'll be fine here. She loves being with all of you — and Jake."

Jake had trotted over to Willow and was nosing her curiously. The dogs were good friends. Neil guessed that the Border collie was wondering why Willow wouldn't roll around with him like she usually did.

"We love having her," said Carole.

Neil exchanged a glance with Emily. They grinned at each other.

"Cool!" said Emily. "We'll have puppies for Christmas!"

"Puppies! Puppies!" said Sarah, wriggling on her chair and nearly knocking over her glass of orange juice. "Will they be born on Christmas Day?"

"They could be," said Glen. "I think it's going to be a race between whether Willow has her pups or Kate has our baby first!"

*   *   *

When dinner was over, Neil and Emily went across to the storeroom to fetch the whelping box. This was a box specially made for dogs about to give birth. It had high, protective sides and an infrared heat lamp to keep the young pups warm. They carried it into the utility room and set it down in the corner farthest from the door, away from any cold drafts.

"We need newspapers to line the bottom," Neil said.

"There are stacks in the cupboard under the stairs," said Emily. "I'll get some."

When she came back, Willow came waddling after her. The little dog sniffed the whelping box curiously as Emily lined the bottom with a thick layer of newspaper. "There you are, Willow," she said. "Nice and cozy."

Neil squatted down beside Willow and fished out a dog treat for her. She sniffed it and gave him a happy look from bright eyes under shaggy white fur. Neil stroked her ears. "You'll be just fine here, girl," he promised her. "Real five-star service from the Puppy Patrol!"

Willow began to investigate the whelping box. Neil was tempting her into the box with some dog treats when Kate appeared in the doorway, with Glen behind her.

"This looks great," she said. "I know Willow's going to be fine." Awkwardly, she bent over and gave her dog a farewell pat. "Be a good girl for Neil and Emily, do you hear?"

Wagging her stumpy tail, Willow looked up at Kate, and gave her hand a swift lick. When Kate went back to the door, the little dog started to follow.

"No, girl," Neil said, taking hold of Willow's collar. "You've got to stay here."

"It won't be for long," Glen said. Neil wasn't sure whether he was trying to comfort Kate or Willow. They both looked sad to be saying good-bye.

As the door of the utility room closed behind Kate and Glen, Willow barked sharply. She stood still for a moment, whining, and then climbed into the whelping box, turned around a couple of times, and settled down with her nose on her paws, watching the door intently.

Emily leaned over to give her a reassuring stroke. "Kate will come and see you," she said, "and you'll be back home before you know it."

Willow's eyes stayed fixed on the door as if she was waiting for Kate to return. Watching the sad little dog, Neil resolved to give their Christmas visitor the best care that King Street Kennels had to offer.

As soon as he got up the next morning, Neil grabbed his digital camera and went downstairs. The kitchen was empty except for Jake in his basket. The young Border collie sprang up and went to stand beside the kitchen door as soon as he saw Neil, his plumy tail waving wildly.

"OK, boy," Neil said. "Hang on a minute."

Quietly, he opened the door of the utility room to look in on Willow. The little white dog was curled up asleep in the whelping box and didn't stir as Neil peered at her around the door. He reached in and took down his jacket.

"Fine," Neil murmured, and closed the door again.

When he let Jake out, he saw that more snow had fallen overnight, covering the courtyard with a fluffy white blanket. Frost sparkled on the surface in the early morning sun.

Already, lines of footprints crisscrossed the courtyard. As Neil fastened his jacket, he saw his dad emerge from Red's Barn with an armful of bedding, then plod through the snow toward Kennel Block One.

"Morning, Dad!" Neil called. "I'm going to take Brutus's picture."

"Don't go in the pen, OK?" Bob called back. "I'll be with you in a minute."

"OK!" Neil crunched across the snow, heading for the rescue center. Jake danced around him, barking joyfully and kicking up snow as he bounded across the yard. Neil shivered as the icy flakes caught him in the face. "Calm down, you crazy dog!" he muttered.

Inside the rescue center he found Bev, the Parkers' other full-time kennel assistant, making up the morning feeds for the rescue dogs. She was a small, slender woman with a lively face. She was wearing jeans tucked into boots and a sheepskin coat over a thick sweater. "Hi," she said. "You're up early."

"I want to take Brutus's picture to put on the web site," Neil explained. "Have you met Brutus? Isn't he a beauty?"

"He's a handsome dog," Bev agreed, pausing to take a look at the Doberman. Brutus was standing near the door of the pen, watching them through the mesh. "But your dad said he's unpredictable. He told me not to open the pen until he gets here."

"Last night he was hungry and scared, that's all. He'll be fine when he settles down," Neil said, leaping to Brutus's defense.

Jake appeared in the doorway and gave himself a vigorous shake, showering icy drops over Neil and Bev. Then he trotted over to Brutus's pen and sniffed cautiously at the Doberman. Brutus lowered his head and the two dogs stood nose to nose.

"Hey, he likes Jake!" said Neil. He went over to the pen, but as soon as Brutus saw him he retreated a couple of paces.

"Steady, boy," Neil said. He fished a dog treat out of his pocket and gave it to Jake, then pushed another tidbit through the mesh in front of Brutus.

The Doberman eyed it suspiciously before darting forward to snatch it up. He took it to the back of the pen to eat.

"Good boy," said Neil. "Come on, have another one." He pushed a second tidbit through the mesh.

Still looking wary, Brutus padded over to take it.

"You're doing fine, boy," Neil said. "It won't be long before —"

Cold air wafted in behind him as the door opened. Brutus snarled, showing his sharp white teeth. He lowered his head threateningly and took a couple of steps backward, stiff-legged.

Neil stared at the dog in alarm, then turned around to see what had upset him so much.

In the doorway stood his dad.

CHAPTER THREE

"**D**ad!" Neil exclaimed. He couldn't understand it. Bob Parker was better at looking after dogs than anyone Neil had ever known. Neil couldn't believe that Brutus had changed so much, just at the sight of him.

"I hope you're being careful," Bob said. He shook his head sadly as he looked at the Doberman, who was still growling fiercely from the back of his pen. "I had hoped he would be settling down by now."

"But he is," Neil protested. "At least, he was."

"That's right," said Bev, who had been watching Brutus closely. "Honestly, Bob, he was nervous with Neil, but not like *this*."

"He was fine until . . ." Neil's voice trailed off.

"Until I came in," Bob finished for him.

Neil nodded.

For a moment, Bob looked upset at the thought that any dog would be frightened of him. But then he shrugged. "Well," he said, "I'm the big ogre who put the muzzle on him. He might need time to get over that. All the same," he added, "*I'm* going to put the food in his pen, not you."

He took the bowls of food and water that Bev had already prepared. Neil opened the pen door. Brutus didn't move as Bob went in and put the bowls down, but he went on growling with a low, throaty sound. He didn't try to take the food until Bob had backed out of the pen and Neil had closed the door again.

"There must be something we can do for him until we find his owner," Neil said.

Bob nodded. "We'll do the best we can. Dobermans are wonderful dogs — loyal and intelligent, and not afraid of anything. Usually. Something bad must have happened to this one. The first thing he'll have to learn is to trust people again."

"You can trust us," Neil said to Brutus. "We'll look after you."

Once he saw that Brutus was eating his breakfast, Bob went out again. Bev fed the other two rescue dogs and started to clean up the work area. "I'm off," she said when she had finished. "There are two new dogs coming in this morning, and I need to clean out the pens in Kennel Block One."

"I'll come and help you after breakfast," Neil said. He knew Bev had to work harder than ever now that Kate wasn't there. "But I want to take a picture of Brutus first to put on the web site."

"Thanks," said Bev. "I could use another pair of hands. The first person to invent a self-cleaning dog pen will make a fortune!" She opened the door and looked back at Neil as she left. "Remember what your dad said. Don't open that door."

After he had taken a picture of Brutus, Neil went back to the house for breakfast. Bob was at the stove, frying bacon and sausages, while Carole sorted through the mail. Emily and Sarah were sitting at the table eating cereal.

Willow was awake now, sitting at Bob's feet with her eyes fixed on the pan. Jake bounded over to Willow and touched noses with her.

"I'm starving," Neil said, pulling off his jacket and stamping his feet on the mat to get rid of the slushy snow.

"Did you take Brutus's picture?" Emily asked him. "I'm going to update the web site after breakfast."

Neil nodded, sliding into his place at the table and pouring himself a bowl of cereal. There were several envelopes beside his bowl.

"Christmas cards!" he said, tearing open the envelopes and spooning cereal into his mouth at the same time. "There's one with an American stamp — it must be from Jane and Richard."

The Parkers' neighbors, Jane and Richard Hammond, had recently left Compton to live in the United States. In the summer, Neil and Emily had visited them and their Border collie Delilah, who was Jake's mom.

"Yes, it is," Neil went on. "Oh, and there's another card inside — just look at that!"

He held out the card for Emily to see. On the front of it was a black-and-white dog wearing a Santa Claus hat, and inside it said, "To Jake with love from Mom." Beside the writing was a paw print. It was from Delilah.

"Hey, Jake, you got a Christmas card!" said Emily.

Jake took no notice. He was much more interested in the bacon and sausages that Bob was dishing onto plates.

"I'm going to make a card for Fudge," Sarah announced.

"Good idea," said Emily. She gave Neil a sharp nudge with her elbow. "And then we're going to make a snow hamster, aren't we, Neil?"

"Can't," Neil mumbled through a mouthful of cornflakes. "I said I'd help Bev."

"Excuses, excuses," Emily said, grinning at him.

"Well, whatever you do, make sure you're finished by lunchtime," Carole said. "This afternoon we're all going to Padsham. You should be able to finish your Christmas shopping there."

"Oh, Mom, do we have to?" Neil protested. "There's so much to do here."

"Yes, you do," said Carole firmly. She started to collect the empty cereal bowls. "Unless you've already bought every single present you need to buy. Tomorrow's Christmas Eve, so this is your last chance."

"OK, OK," Neil said. He began wolfing down his bacon, pausing only to slip scraps to Jake and Willow under the table. "Come on, Em. Let's get to work on the web site."

In the office, Neil put the picture of Brutus up on the King Street Kennels' web site, and then Emily typed in a description of the Doberman and the details of where he had been found. "You know," she said, with her fingers poised above the keyboard, "I'm not so sure about this."

"What do you mean?" Neil asked.

"Well . . . do we really *want* to find Brutus's owner? Look how scared and wild he is — maybe he's like that because his owner treated him badly.

"We don't know that," Neil argued. "He might have been fine until he got lost."

Emily shrugged and started typing again. "Maybe." She didn't sound convinced. "But if somebody does come to claim Brutus, I think we should check up really carefully before we hand him over."

Neil had to admit that his sister was right.

Something had made Brutus mistrustful and angry. Neil wouldn't be satisfied until they found out what it was.

By lunchtime, Neil had helped Bev clean out the pens for the new arrivals, built a whole family of snow hamsters with Emily and Sarah, and taken some of the boarding dogs for a run in the exercise field. By the time he returned the last of them, a highly excitable cocker spaniel, to its pen, he figured he had earned his lunch.

As Neil opened the kitchen door he almost tripped over Willow, who was peering out. "No, girl," he said, nudging her gently back inside with one foot. "It's way too cold for you out there. You stay in the warm and look after those pups!" He bent down and rubbed her swollen belly.

"She's been a bit restless this morning," Carole said, looking up from the copy of the *Compton News* she had spread over the kitchen table. "I think she misses Kate and Glen. Your dad called Mike Turner and he's going to come over and give her a checkup later on."

"Great," said Neil. He peeled off his wet, woolly gloves. His fingers were so cold he could hardly feel them and he rubbed them together vigorously. "We'll look after you, Willow. Don't you worry about a thing."

Almost as if she understood him, Willow perked up a little and her stumpy tail started wagging. She trotted across the kitchen and buried her nose in her water bowl.

"I'm sure she's fine, really," Carole said, "but —" She broke off as the kitchen door crashed open and Emily hurtled in. "Emily!"

"Sorry, mom." Emily waved a piece of paper she was clutching in her hand. "Neil, look at this. It's an e-mail about Brutus — I printed it out."

"From his owner?" Neil asked, grabbing at the paper.

"No, from somebody who knows him. Read it."

Neil looked at the e-mail. It read:

I think Brutus is the dog who used to live next door to us. His owner has gone away. If you call me, I'll tell you all about him.

There was a Padsham phone number and the name Jackie Meadows.

"I'm going to call right now," Neil said.

"Don't be long, then," said Carole. "I'm just about to serve lunch."

"Five minutes, Mom — OK?" When his mom nodded, Neil went out to the phone in the hall and Emily followed him. He dialed the number printed at the bottom of the e-mail. The phone was answered almost at once.

A woman's voice said, "Yes?"

"Hello," Neil said. "Is this Jackie Meadows?"

"No, it's her mother. Who's calling, please?"

"I'm Neil Parker, from King Street Kennels in Compton." Neil explained about the e-mail from Jackie. "Could I speak to her, please?"

"I'll go and get her," the woman said. "Please hold on."

Neil waited, fizzing with impatience.

"What did they say?" Emily asked. "What's going on?"

"She's getting Jackie," Neil told her, as a voice at

the other end of the phone said, "Hello, this is Jackie Meadows."

"Hi," said Neil. "I'm Neil Parker from King Street Kennels. You sent us an e-mail about Brutus."

"That's right," Jackie said. Neil thought she sounded friendly. "I often check your site. I really love dogs."

"You said you know all about Brutus," Neil prompted, barely able to contain his eagerness. It looked like they were about to solve the mystery of Brutus's past.

"I'm sure it's the same dog," Jackie told him. "His owner used to live next door to us, but he went away a couple of weeks ago — he got a new job in Manchester. The house is empty now."

"That would explain why I couldn't get through on the phone," Neil said.

"I thought he must have taken Brutus with him," Jackie went on. "There's been no sign of him around here. I was really surprised when I saw his picture on your web site."

"We found him hiding behind the garbage cans at our school," Neil said. "He was starving, and he looks really thin."

"Oh, no!" The voice at the other end of the phone sounded indignant. "And he's such a good dog. He doesn't deserve that."

"So, what —" Neil was interrupted by Emily grabbing his arm.

"What is she saying? Does she know our Brutus?" she demanded.

At the same moment, Carole's voice came from the kitchen. "Lunch!"

"Look," Neil said to Jackie, "I can't really talk now. Would it be OK if I came over to see you?" He remembered that his mom had threatened to take them Christmas shopping in Padsham that afternoon. "Will you be in after lunch?"

"Yes, that would be fine," Jackie said. "We live on Orchard Road in Padsham — number 12. It's just past the swimming pool."

"Oh, I know where that is." Neil and Emily had often gone swimming in the Padsham pool. "We'll see you later, then."

He put the phone down and turned to Emily. "We're going to see Jackie this afternoon," he announced.

Emily's face split into a grin. "Great."

"She sounds really nice," Neil added as they headed for the kitchen. "And she said Brutus is a good dog. So it doesn't sound as if he's always been savage."

"Yes," Emily said thoughtfully. "Maybe this afternoon we'll find out what happened to change him."

CHAPTER FOUR

That afternoon, Carole drove Neil, Emily, and Sarah into Padsham in the King Street Kennels Range Rover. They arranged to meet a couple of hours later, which would give Neil and Emily just enough time to visit Jackie Meadows and finish off the last of their Christmas shopping.

The center of Padsham was bright with Christmas lights. The sound of carols came from loudspeakers on a stall where the local Rotary club was collecting donations for children's charities. All the shop windows were hung with glittery decorations and sprayed with fake snow.

Neil and Emily headed out of the town center, past the swimming pool. Though the snow had stopped falling, an icy wind swept down the road toward them, stinging their faces. Neil kept his head down and pulled up the hood of his jacket. Beside him, Jake trotted along the slushy pavement as if he didn't mind the cold at all.

"I wish I was a dog!" Neil muttered. "I'd have a built-in fur coat!"

Number 12, Orchard Road, turned out to be a modern red-brick house. The snow in the front garden was well trodden and a lopsided snowman stood in the middle. A Christmas tree with flashing lights stood inside the front window.

Next to it, number 14 was dark and quiet. There were no curtains in the windows, and the snow in the garden was undisturbed. A real estate agent's board that read FOR SALE stood beside the gate.

"That must be where Brutus lived," said Emily.

Neil pushed open the gate of number 12 and led the way up the path. Almost as soon as he pressed the bell the door was opened, as if someone had been looking out for them.

In the doorway stood a girl about his own age. She was shorter than Neil, with frizzy brown hair in pigtails. She wore jeans and a red sweatshirt with a reindeer on the front.

"Hi," she said, smiling brightly. "You must be Neil Parker. I'm Jackie. Come in."

Neil stepped into the hall, glad to be out of the cold wind. "Yes, I'm Neil. This is my sister Emily — and Jake."

Jackie said hello to Emily and bent down to talk
to Jake. Neil noticed that she didn't make any sud-
den movements and that she held out her hand for
Jake to sniff before she tried to pat him. Neil could
see that Jackie was someone who really understood
dogs.

"Have you got a dog of your own?" he asked.

Jackie shook her head regretfully. "I'd love one,
but —" She broke off as a door opened behind her
and a woman came out into the hall.

Neil guessed that she must be Jackie's mom; she

looked exactly like an older version of Jackie, except that her frizzy hair was cut short. A small boy with blond hair was peering out curiously from behind her legs.

"You must be the Parkers," said Mrs. Meadows warmly. "Jackie, why don't you take them into the front room? Would you like some hot chocolate?"

"Yes, please!" Neil and Emily said together.

The woman vanished again and Jackie opened the door beside her and showed Neil and Emily into the cozy room. Another small boy, identical to the first, was sitting in the middle of the carpet in a nest of Christmas wrapping paper, winding ribbon around himself.

"No, Ben!" Jackie swooped on him and started to unwind the ribbon. Laughing, she added, "That's to wrap presents with, not you! Or should I wrap you up and send you through the mail?"

"Mail," the little boy agreed, with a big grin.

Jackie untangled the last of the ribbon and steered Ben toward the door. "Go into the kitchen and play with Nicky. Mom might have something for you."

"Cookie," Ben said hopefully and trotted out.

Still smiling, Jackie sank into a chair, then started to wind up the ribbon. "Little brothers! I love them to pieces, but they drive me crazy. And that's why we don't have a dog. Mom and Dad think it wouldn't be safe until the twins are a bit older."

"We've always had dogs," Neil said.

"And we've got a little sister, too," Emily added.

Jackie shrugged. "Well, maybe you can persuade my mom."

We might try that, Neil thought as he took off his jacket and sat down. It looked like Jackie was part of a big, friendly family. And, in Neil's opinion, a family wasn't complete without a dog. "OK," he said. "Tell us about Brutus."

"Well . . ." Jackie leaned forward, starting to look more serious. "Our next door neighbor was a guy called Simon Soames. He worked nights as an engineer at the local radio station. Last year, his girlfriend gave him Brutus as a Christmas present."

"Uh-oh!" Neil rolled his eyes. "I can guess what you're going to say. This Simon Soames had no idea his girlfriend was going to give him a puppy, right?"

"Right," said Jackie. She sounded angry. "It was a big surprise."

Emily let out a snort of indignation. "People are so thoughtless! Owning a dog is a *huge* responsibility. You should never give one as a present without making sure the owner knows what they're taking on."

"So true!" Jackie agreed. "Anyway, at first I thought it would be OK. Brutus was a cute little pup and Simon and his girlfriend — Marilyn — spent hours playing with him in the garden. The problems started when Brutus got bigger."

Before Jackie could tell them what the problems

were, the door opened and Mrs. Meadows came into the room with a tray. It held mugs of hot chocolate, a plate of mince pie, and another of chocolate-chip cookies.

"Great!" said Neil. "Thanks, Mrs. Meadows."

"It's my pleasure," said Mrs. Meadows, setting the tray down on the coffee table in front of the fire. "Especially if you can do something to help Brutus. I've been really worried about that dog."

Just then a crash sounded from somewhere in the hall. "Nicky! Ben!" Mrs. Meadows called and hurried out.

Jackie handed out the mugs of hot chocolate. Jake got up from the hearth-rug and came to look interestedly at the plates.

"Can I give him a cookie?" Jackie asked.

Neil started to fish out his dog treats, then put them away again. "Just one," he said. "After all, it *is* Christmas."

Jake crunched the chocolate-chip cookie enthusiastically, but he was well trained enough to realize that there wouldn't be any more. He made himself comfortable on the rug again.

"He's great," Jackie said admiringly. "Oh, I do wish we had a dog! Mom and Dad say when the boys go to school we can get one, but that's years away."

"Go on about Brutus," Neil prompted her.

"OK, where was I? Oh, yes, when Brutus got bigger . . . Well, Simon didn't have a lot of free time to give to Brutus. He slept during the day and worked at night and in his spare time he went out with Marilyn. He seemed to think that it was enough just to feed Brutus and leave him in the yard."

"All by himself?" exclaimed Emily. "That's *awful*! Dobermans need to be around people and other dogs. I've been reading about them in my dog magazines. They aren't happy if they're left alone."

"I used to talk to him over the fence," said Jackie. "And after a while I asked Simon if I could take him for walks. He said I could, because Brutus's barking disturbed him when he was trying to sleep. Simon couldn't see that the barking was *his* fault."

"He sounds like a real genius," Neil said sarcastically.

"Well, he was ignorant about dogs," said Jackie. "Anyway, I used to walk Brutus most days after school. He had a basket and his leash in the garden shed, so I used to take him out whenever I could. I —"

"You mean he wasn't allowed into the house?" Emily interrupted, her eyes wide with shock.

Jackie shook her head. "I think Simon was doing his best to forget that he even had a dog. Which meant that, apart from me, Brutus hardly saw anybody. When I went over there he used to get so excited, he'd bark his head off and start jumping up. I taught him to sit, but he wouldn't do it for Simon. Simon would just yell at Brutus, and that didn't do any good at all."

Neil nodded. "Dogs don't understand if you shout. They get upset."

"The barking got so bad that the neighbors started to complain," Jackie went on. "So Simon bought this really tight muzzle and made Brutus wear it."

Neil and Emily exchanged a glance. "So *that's* why Brutus always growls at Dad!" said Emily.

Neil explained to Jackie how Bob had muzzled Brutus while they got him safely to the rescue center, and how Brutus was more mistrustful of Bob than anyone else.

"You can't blame him," Jackie said. "And the muzzle wasn't the worst thing, either." She hesitated, took a gulp of her hot chocolate, and went on. "I noticed a couple of times that Brutus looked kind of battered, and once he was bleeding from his ear. I asked Simon what had happened and he said he'd gotten into a fight with another dog." She made a disbelieving noise. "I'd just like to know when Brutus ever had a chance to fight with other dogs. It wasn't when he was with me, that's for sure."

"You're saying *Simon* hurt him?" Neil asked. He couldn't remember ever feeling so disgusted. No wonder poor Brutus was nervous and aggressive.

Jackie shrugged. "If you can think of a better explanation, tell me what it is." She handed out the last of the mince pie and the three of them sat munching.

Neil thought over what he had heard. His initial

determination to find Brutus's owner had changed into a fierce resolve not to give the Doberman back to Simon Soames, whatever happened. Not that it sounded as if Simon would *want* him back. "So what happened when Simon left?" he asked.

"Let me show you something," Jackie said. She stood up, brushing pastry crumbs off her sweatshirt. "Put your coats on. It's in the backyard."

Neil and Emily picked up their jackets and followed Jackie along the hall into the kitchen, with Jake trotting at their heels. Ben and Nicky were playing with colorful clay at the kitchen table, while Mrs. Meadows stirred something in a pan on the stove.

"We're just going out for a minute, Mom," Jackie said, taking a thick padded jacket from a peg by the back door.

Mrs. Meadows nodded and smiled.

Jackie led the way into the snow-covered yard, to the fence that separated it from number 14. She pointed to the fence at the bottom of number 14's yard. "Do you see that?"

The daylight was fading, but Neil could just make out that one of the planks in the fence was hanging loose, with a space at the bottom big enough for a determined dog to wriggle through.

"Brutus ran away!" said Emily.

"Can't say I blame him," Neil added.

"He did it once before, about a month ago," Jackie

explained. "I think he was so bored in the backyard that he pulled the plank out himself and went out into the street. That time he ended up in a yard farther down the road and the people there brought him back. They were furious — he'd dug up some of their precious plants!"

"I bet Simon wasn't too thrilled," Neil said grimly, dreading to think how Soames might have punished the frustrated dog.

"You can say that again. But he didn't fix the fence. I bet he was hoping that one day Brutus would wander off and not come back."

"But that's so irresponsible!" Neil exploded. "If he didn't want Brutus, he could have found him another home. He could have brought him to us at King Street. We would have looked after him."

"Simon couldn't have cared less," said Jackie. She

shivered. "It's freezing out here. Let's go back in-side."

They crunched their way across the snowy patio and back into the kitchen. Mrs. Meadows turned away from her cooking as they came in. "I can't tell you how relieved I am that someone is helping that poor dog," she said. "It's been worrying me for months. Even when I thought he'd gone off to Manchester with Simon, I couldn't get him out of my head."

"Did Simon even try to take Brutus with him?" Neil asked.

"I don't know," said Jackie. "Simon got a better job in Manchester, so he moved there a few weeks ago. Brutus disappeared about the same time, so I assumed Simon had taken him."

"Well, he never said he wasn't going to," said Mrs. Meadows, taking her pan off the heat. "Simon definitely told me he'd found an apartment and —"

"But you can't keep a Doberman in an apartment!" Emily was outraged. "They're big dogs. They need space."

"I bet Brutus didn't run away again," said Neil. "I bet Simon just left him behind."

"Well, I'm sorry to say it, but I wouldn't be at all surprised," said Mrs. Meadows. "I just hope that now you'll be able to find him a really good home with people who care about him."

"We'll certainly try," said Neil.

"I'll give you Simon's new address and phone number," Mrs. Meadows said, wiping her hands on a towel and picking up a pad and pencil from the kitchen counter. "I suppose you'll have to check that he really doesn't want Brutus."

As she scribbled down the information, an idea began to grow in Neil's mind. Trying to sound casual, he said, "Would you like to come over and visit Brutus? I bet he'd like to see some old friends."

"Can we, Mom?" Jackie said, beaming. "I've really missed him."

"Well, I don't see why not." Mrs. Meadows smiled as she gave Neil the piece of paper with Simon Soames's address on it. "You'd like to go and see Brutus, wouldn't you?" she asked the twins.

"Big dog," said Ben solemnly.

"That's right," Emily said. "We've got lots of dogs for you to see."

Ben's twin, Nicky, started bouncing up and down and banging the table with a wooden spoon. "See lots of dogs!" he agreed.

Neil exchanged a sympathetic glance with Jackie. Ben and Nicky were even more noisy than his little sister Sarah! "Come any time," he said. "Best to give us a call first, though."

He and Emily said good-bye to the Meadows and set off back to the town center. There was just time to finish their Christmas shopping before they had to meet their mom.

"That was a good idea," said Emily. "Inviting them

to come and visit. I really like them. And I bet it'll help Brutus to see his friends again."

"That's not all," Neil grinned. "Brutus can't go back to Simon, right?"

"Right!" Emily agreed firmly.

"So he needs a good home. Well, I think we just found one," said Neil confidently.

Emily paused, her mouth open with surprise. "The Meadows? But you heard what Jackie said. Their mom and dad won't let them have a dog until the boys are bigger."

"Then we'll just have to hope they change their minds — won't we, boy?" Neil said to Jake.

Jake let out an approving bark.

"Jackie and her family are the perfect owners for Brutus," Neil went on. "They just don't know it yet!"

CHAPTER FIVE

When the Parkers arrived back at King Street Kennels, another car was already parked there.

"Mike's here!" Neil exclaimed.

He and Emily piled out of the Range Rover and ran up the steps to the front door and into the house. Through the open door of the utility room Neil could hear voices — his dad's and the vet's.

"I've got no worries about Willow at all, physically," Mike Turner was saying. "She's a healthy dog and she's in great shape to have her pups."

"That's good to hear," said Bob.

Neil went into the utility room with Emily behind him. Mike was squatting on the floor beside Willow, who was lying on her side in the whelping box. He grinned up at Neil and Emily as they came in and beckoned them over. "Here," he said to Neil, holding out a stethoscope. "Come and listen to this."

Neil fitted the hooks into his ears and Mike held the end to Willow's stomach. Neil could hear a very faint, rhythmic sound. "What is it?" he asked.

"Willow's pups," said Mike with a grin. "That's their heartbeats."

"Wow!" said Neil. He could hardly believe he was actually listening to the tiny, living creatures inside Willow.

The little white dog turned her head to see what

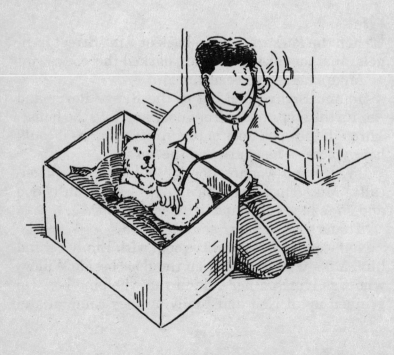

he was doing, and then turned away again. Neil thought she still looked listless, not the bright, happy dog she usually was.

He passed the stethoscope to Emily so that she could have a turn and watched an incredulous smile spread across her face as she listened to the muffled sounds. "That's so cool!" she breathed.

"As I said, Bob," Mike went on, "I've got no real worries about Willow's health, but she does seem a bit depressed."

"I think she misses Kate and Glen," Emily said, handing the stethoscope back to Mike. "Let's invite them over for dinner — we can, can't we, Mom?" Emily twisted around to look at Carole, who had just appeared in the doorway of the utility room.

Carole agreed that was a great idea and Emily went off to phone Kate and Glen.

Mike Turner gave Willow a farewell pat and started to pack up his equipment. "See that she gets plenty to eat," he said to Neil, "but don't let her stuff herself. If she overeats, she'll have more trouble delivering her pups. And gentle exercise is good. She'll know how much she feels like doing."

"Will do!" said Neil. "You can rely on the Puppy Patrol!" He bent down to ruffle Willow's wiry coat. "Don't worry, girl. It won't be long now."

"How did things go this afternoon?" Bob asked Neil as they went back into the kitchen.

Neil launched into the story of how Brutus had

been mistreated by his previous owner. By the time he had finished, Bob was frowning thoughtfully.

"That certainly explains a lot," he said. "It's tough for Brutus — his temperament could be permanently spoiled by a bad start like that."

"I don't believe it!" Emily said angrily. "Brutus is great — he just needs proper care, that's all."

Bob smiled. "You might be right. We'll do what we can, at any rate."

"Would you like me to take a look at him?" Mike Turner offered.

"Yes, please," Bob replied. "I'm pretty sure there's nothing wrong with him, though, apart from lack of food while he was living on the streets."

"A checkup will do no harm," said Mike. "And if you want to take this further, it might be helpful to have my opinion of the dog's condition."

Bob scratched his beard. "That's true."

"Do you think we should do something about Simon Soames?" Neil asked. "Mrs. Meadows gave me his new address and phone number. Do you want to call him?"

"I don't think so," said Bob. "The person I want to call is Terri McCall. I think the SPCA should know what's going on." He glanced at his watch. "I should just be able to catch her. Neil, you take Mike out to see Brutus."

Neil fished in his pocket for the piece of paper Mrs.

Meadows had given him and handed it to his dad. Then he led Mike out to the rescue center.

Snow started to fall again as they crossed the courtyard, but inside the rescue center it was invitingly warm. Brutus was lying down when Neil and Mike went in, but he leaped to his feet as they approached the pen and retreated to the back wall.

"He's a fine-looking fellow," Mike observed. "Let's take a closer look, shall we?"

Neil opened the door of the pen. He knew his dad wouldn't mind him going in when Mike was with him.

Brutus didn't growl or show any other signs of aggression, but Neil could see he was trembling. He fished in his pocket for a dog treat and dropped it on the floor by his boots. After a short hesitation, Brutus came up to him and took it.

"He's starting to trust you, at least," said Mike. "Can you hold him for me while I examine him? We'll muzzle him first if you like."

"Oh, no," Neil said. "Nobody's going to put a muzzle on Brutus again — are they, boy?" He crouched down beside the Doberman and put a hand on his flank. He could feel how tense the dog was. "Take it easy, boy," he said soothingly. "Mike's just going to take a look at you."

Neil kept one hand on Brutus's collar and talked to him as the vet gave him a thorough examination.

As he stroked the sleek black-and-tan coat, Neil could feel Brutus starting to relax.

"Well," Mike said at last, sitting back on his heels, "I don't think I can tell you anything you don't already know. There's nothing serious wrong with him. He's been pretty hungry for a while, but he's getting over that. There are one or two small scars — here, look, and here." He gently tilted Brutus's head toward the light. "I doubt they're dog bites. My guess would be that someone hit him with something thin, like a stick."

Neil felt sick. "I'd like to hit Simon Soames with a stick!"

"The SPCA will take care of Soames, I bet," said Mike. "Hitting any dog is a horrible thing to do, but Dobermans in particular can't stand it. It confuses them and makes them angry." He gave Brutus a pat. "Never mind, boy. You're in good hands now."

Neil took out another dog treat and dropped it on the floor in front of Brutus. The Doberman crunched it and gave Neil a bright, alert look, as if he wanted more. Neil suddenly felt hopeful. He'd never seen Brutus look quite so friendly before.

He took out another tidbit and, daringly, held it out on the palm of his hand. Brutus nuzzled him, his lips feeling soft and velvety, and took the treat gently.

Neil patted him. "That's right, boy. You know you're OK now, don't you?"

Brutus flopped down on the ground again, his head raised and alert. He already looked like a different dog from the one Neil and Emily had found poking around the school.

"If he goes on like this, you won't have any trouble finding him a new home," said Mike.

Neil grinned. "I know! And I've got just the people in mind!"

When Kate and Glen arrived for dinner, Neil could see how tired Kate was looking. She was moving very slowly and awkwardly — just like Willow, who came padding out to greet her.

"I really miss her," Kate confessed, reaching down to ruffle Willow's ears. "But I know she's in the right place here. I couldn't even bend down to put her food on the floor!"

While they ate, Neil told Kate and Glen about Brutus and what he had heard about the Doberman's previous owner.

"People like that shouldn't be allowed to keep a dog," said Glen, who was involved with a local animal rights group. "Brutus will be lucky if he's not damaged permanently."

"He's a great dog!" Neil insisted. "He's going to be fine."

When the meal was over, Kate made herself comfortable on the sofa in the living room, with Willow tucked next to her. She stroked the little dog's fur lovingly.

"Why don't you go and see this new dog?" she suggested to Glen. "Willow and I will just enjoy each other's company for a while."

Neil and Glen went out to the rescue center. Brutus raised his head as they went up to the pen, but for the first time he had enough confidence not to retreat to the back wall.

Neil could see the admiration in Glen's eyes as he studied the powerful Doberman. Brutus's black-and-tan coat gleamed and his eyes shone with intelligence as he looked steadily back at them.

"Hi there, boy," Glen said, slipping a dog treat through the mesh. "It beats me how anyone could mistreat a fantastic dog like that," he added.

Neil shrugged. He'd given up trying to understand people like Simon Soames.

"Well, Brutus," said Glen. The young Doberman pricked his ears as if he was listening. "You've got nothing to worry about now. You've got the Puppy Patrol looking after you!"

When Neil and Glen went back to the house, they found Kate and Willow peacefully asleep in front of the fire.

Glen shook his wife's shoulder gently to wake her. "Come on, Kate, it's time to go home."

Kate blinked and yawned and ran her hand sadly over Willow's head. "I really hate leaving her."

"It won't be for much longer now," Glen said comfortingly, patting Kate's enormous tummy. "I'm just waiting to see who's going to win this race!"

The next day was Christmas Eve. Neil and Emily were putting the finishing touches on the tree in the living room when the phone rang. A moment later, Neil heard his mom's voice. "Neil, it's for you."

"Hi, it's Jackie," said a cheerful voice as he picked up the phone. "Listen, Mom and Dad want to come over to Compton to see Grandma, and we thought we could drop by King Street — if that's OK with you."

"That's fine," said Neil. "Come as soon as you want." He went back into the living room to tell Emily the news.

His sister had just draped the last piece of tinsel over the tree and was standing back to admire the effect. "Great," she said when Neil told her his news. "Are you going to ask them if they'll take Brutus?"

"I'm not sure," Neil said. "I don't want to rush them, but they might not come here again. I think I'll just play it by ear."

Neil still wasn't sure when Jackie arrived with her mom and a tall, dark-haired man who introduced himself as Jackie's father, Alan.

"We left Nicky and Ben with Grandma," Jackie explained.

"I'm sure the dogs wouldn't scare them," Emily said.

Jackie giggled. "No, but *they* might scare the dogs!"

Neil showed Mr. and Mrs. Meadows into the office to say hello to Carole, who was working on the computer, and then he and Emily took them to see Brutus.

"What a fantastic place!" Jackie exclaimed as Neil led the way into the rescue center. "And there's Brutus — hi there, boy! Do you remember me?"

She hardly needed to ask. Brutus had been lying in his pen, dozing, but as soon as he heard the sound of her voice he leaped to his feet and let out a joyous bark. A second later, to Neil's amazement, the dog reared up against the mesh, his paws splayed out, panting eagerly as Jackie came toward him.

Neil couldn't believe the change in Brutus. This was the first time he had ever come up to the mesh by himself, without someone coaxing him. For a nervous and unhappy dog, he suddenly seemed eager and friendly.

That settles it, Neil said to himself. *Jackie* has *to be the right owner for Brutus.*

Jackie went up to Brutus, a delighted smile on her face, and reached out to rub his nose through the mesh. "He looks fine," she said to Neil.

"You should have seen him a couple of days ago," Neil said. "He was really thin and you could see all his ribs. But we've been feeding him well. Mike Turner, the vet, says there's nothing wrong with him."

"I'm so relieved!" said Mrs. Meadows. "Before you came to see us, I hadn't been able to get the poor creature out of my mind. Even when I thought he was with Simon, I was worried that he wouldn't be properly taken care of."

"Horrible man!" said Jackie. "Never mind," she added to Brutus. "You won't have to go back to him ever again!"

Neil handed Jackie a dog treat and she offered it to Brutus through the mesh. The young Doberman took it gently and his tail started to wag. Neil stared. In all Brutus's time at King Street, he had never wagged his tail before.

"So what happens now?" Mr. Meadows asked. "Will you be able to find him a new home?"

"Oh, yes," said Emily confidently. "His details are on our web site, and after Christmas I'm going to ask Jake Fielding if he'll put something in the *Compton News*. We're sure to find someone who wants him."

Neil looked at Brutus, who was sniffing happily at Jackie's hands. "He can stay here until we find the right owners for him," he said. *And with any luck,* he added silently, *that won't be very long*. He paused while Jackie went on petting Brutus, and then thought, *Go for it!*

"Of course," Neil went on, "the people who take him will have to understand what he went through. He'll need a lot of care and love. I think you could do a great job, if you wanted to. He already loves Jackie — you can see he does."

Jackie spun around, her face alight. "Mom, Dad — can we?"

Mr. and Mrs. Meadows exchanged a thoughtful look, and for a minute Neil thought they were going to say yes.

Then Mrs. Meadows slowly shook her head. "I'm sorry. If it was just the three of us . . . but I can't be sure that Brutus would be safe with the twins. They're too little to understand about being careful with him."

"I'd look after him, Mom," Jackie said.

"And we'll stay in touch," Emily added. "We'll give you all the help we can."

"That's not the point," Jackie's dad said. "The point is that Brutus has had a really bad start in life, and I don't think we're the right people to take him on."

"But —" Neil began.

"No, Neil," Mr. Meadows interrupted. He sounded genuinely sorry. "We're all fond of Brutus, but our children's safety has to come first. It's too much of a risk." He touched his wife's sleeve, indicating that they should leave.

All the happiness had drained out of Jackie's face. There were tears in her eyes as she rubbed Brutus's head one last time. "Good-bye, boy," she whispered. Then she turned away and walked out of the rescue center with her head down.

Her parents followed.

Mrs. Meadows paused to say, "We're really sorry." She squeezed Neil's arm and smiled at him.

Emily went with them to show them out, but Neil stayed with Brutus. Once Jackie had gone, the young dog lay down again. He looked sad, too. He put his nose on his paws and kept his eyes fixed on the door, as if he was waiting for Jackie to come back.

He perked up when the door opened again, but it was only Emily. She was shaking her head. "They're such nice people," she said.

"I know," said Neil. "I just can't understand why they won't see that Brutus is the dog for them."

Emily shrugged. "They're worried about their children."

"But Brutus isn't dangerous!" Neil protested. "I know he isn't. Jackie's parents just won't believe it. And you know what?" he added. "We'll have the same problem with anyone else who comes to look at Brutus. We'll *have* to tell them all about his past. And then they'll expect him to be dangerous as well." Neil stared gloomily through the mesh at the homeless dog. "It's not going to be as easy as we thought. Maybe no one will want him at all."

CHAPTER SIX

"There!" Carole Parker said as she put the last gift-wrapped present under the tree. "All ready for tomorrow." She started ticking items off on her fingers. "I've stuffed the turkey, I've made another batch of mince pies — where did the last ones go, Neil? — I've iced the cake . . ."

"I went out and cut the holly," Neil said in an injured tone. Emily had eaten just as many mince pies as he had. "And washed the dishes after lunch."

"*We* washed the dishes after lunch," Emily reminded him. "I'm sure everything's ready, Mom."

"It had better be." Carole glanced at her watch. "Let's see if your dad's got dinner ready. And don't forget you've got to stay awake for Midnight Mass!"

As they trooped into the kitchen, the phone rang.

Neil picked it up. "King Street Kennels. Can I help you?"

"Hi, Neil." It was Terri McCall, the local SPCA officer.

"Hi!" Neil said eagerly. "Have you done anything about Brutus's owner?"

"I certainly have," Terri said. "I gave the Manchester SPCA office all the details, along with Simon Soames's new address, and they decided to hand everything over to the local police." Her voice grew serious. "Mr. Soames will be getting a visitor soon, and it won't be Santa Claus."

"That's great news," said Neil. "I'll tell Dad."

"Thanks — and thanks for your help, Neil."

"No problem," said Neil. "Merry Christmas!"

"Merry Christmas to you!" said Terri, and hung up.

The bells of Compton Parish Church were ringing as Bob Parker steered the Range Rover into the church parking lot. All the Parkers were bundled up in coats and scarves, and Sarah was bouncing up and down in excitement because, for the first time ever, she was being allowed to stay up for Midnight Mass. She had insisted on wearing her sparkly angel costume from the preschool Nativity play; Neil hoped no one would notice it under her thick coat. Little sisters could be *so* embarrassing!

The night was clear and cold. A million stars twinkled above them and thick snow glittered on the gravestones. The door to the church stood open, shedding warm yellow candlelight onto the path.

Neil thought it looked as if half of Compton was walking through the churchyard. Within a couple of minutes, he had said hello to Sergeant Moorhead, Mr. Hamley and his wife Rachel, and Dr. Harvey, who was with an elderly lady who, Neil guessed, was his mother.

Farther away, Neil spotted his classmate Hasheem Lindon with his sister Rehana and their parents. Emily darted off to wish a Merry Christmas to her best friend Julie Baker. Neil was just waving to Mrs. Smedley from the newsstand when he heard a voice behind him.

"Merry Christmas, all of you!"

It was Mike Turner.

"Merry Christmas, Mike!" Neil said.

"I'll be on call over Christmas," Mike said as they reached the church entrance. "If you need any help with Willow, just give me a ring on my cell phone."

"Fine, we'll do that," Bob said. "I'm not expecting any trouble, but it's good to know you're available."

"You're not on your own over Christmas, are you?" Carole asked anxiously.

"No, I'm going to my sister's," Mike said. "Don't worry. She always cooks a delicious Christmas dinner!"

They went into the church. Emily gasped. "It's so beautiful!" she exclaimed, gazing around her.

Neil had to agree. Every corner of the church was lit by candles — in the pews, on the altar, and in a row of chandeliers above the central aisle. At the far end was a huge Christmas tree hung with silver foil stars, and near the entrance was a Christmas crib.

The organ started to play as the Parkers crammed into a pew. Neil got ready to sing his heart out. Even if he did have a voice like a dog with kennel cough, nobody minded at Christmas!

The reverend, Gavin Thorpe, was standing beside the pulpit, beaming at everyone. Neil was used to seeing him with his black Labrador, Jet, at his heels. He thought it was too bad that Jet couldn't be with Gavin now. Neil would have liked to bring Jake, although he had to admit that Midnight Mass would probably be a bit too crowded if everyone brought their pets along as well.

But when the service was over and the Parkers were lining up with everyone else to shake hands with Gavin on the way out, Neil saw that Jet had appeared from somewhere and was sitting beside his owner.

As soon as he was close enough, Neil fished out a dog treat and bent down to give it to Jet. The Labrador looked alert and happy and he had a Christmas ornament tied to his collar.

"Hi there, Jet," said Neil. "Where did you appear from?"

"He's been waiting for me in the vestry," Gavin explained. "I thought he might be lonely all by himself in the rectory."

"He behaved very well," Carole said. "No one would have known he was there."

"You're a great dog, Jet," Neil said, rumpling the Labrador's ears. "And you have a great Christmas, do you hear?"

Jet thumped his tail on the flagstones as if in agreement and gave Neil's hand a lick. Neil stroked

his smooth head once more and hurried after his
mom and dad.

By the time the Parkers got back to King Street,
Sarah was yawning and hardly able to keep her eyes
open. Carole took her up to bed while Bob, Neil, and
Emily did a final check of the kennel blocks and the
rescue center.

Neil offered to take a look at Brutus, who was all
on his own now that the other two rescue dogs had
been picked up by their new families. As Neil came
in, Brutus raised his head, gave Neil a drowsy look,
and settled down again.

"Have a Merry Christmas, Brutus," Neil said softly.
"And a Happy New Year — I'll make sure of that."

He was letting himself out of the rescue center
again when he heard a loud barking coming from the
house. "That's Jake!" he exclaimed.

Neil dashed across the courtyard and through the
back door. The barking continued. The kitchen was
in darkness. Neil switched on the light and saw Jake
standing in the doorway to the utility room, barking
his head off.

"Jake!" Neil exclaimed. "What is it, boy?" He
crouched down to pat the Border collie. Jake stopped
barking and whined softly. Neil looked past him into
the utility room, where Willow lay in the whelping
box.

One look was enough.

Neil dashed out again and almost collided with Bob, who was returning from Kennel Block One.

"Dad!" Neil gasped. "Come quick! It's Willow — she's having her pups."

CHAPTER SEVEN

"**C**alm down," said Bob. "No need to panic. Let's go and take a look."

He went indoors, and Neil followed him, along with Emily, who had just appeared from Kennel Block Two. Jake settled down near the door of the utility room, his ears pricked as if he understood what was going on.

Neil paused to pat him. "Well done, boy. You warned us, didn't you?"

Willow was shifting restlessly in the whelping box. She was panting rapidly, and she kept turning to lick her hindquarters. As Neil watched, a strong muscular ripple passed over her body.

Bob bent down and checked her gently. "She's well

66

into the second stage of labor," he reported. "Emily, you'll find the things we need in that cupboard — could you get them out for me, please?"

Emily hurried across to fetch the towels and other equipment that Carole had gotten ready as soon as Willow arrived.

Meanwhile, Bob gave his hands a thorough washing. "You should find a hot water bottle in there as well," he said to Emily. "Fill it for me, please — not too hot — and wrap it in a blanket."

While Emily disappeared into the kitchen, Neil went over to Willow and crouched down to stroke the top of her head gently. Willow licked his hand. "You're doing just fine, girl," Neil told her. "Those pups will be here before you know it."

Another powerful ripple ran across Willow's swollen abdomen. Neil knew that meant the first pup was passing down the birth canal, getting ready to be born.

Neil had watched Delilah giving birth to Jake and the rest of the litter, and he'd seen Mr. Hamley's Dalmatian Dotty having her pups, so he knew what to expect, but he still felt so excited he could hardly breathe.

"Come on, girl, push," Neil encouraged Willow. "You can do it!"

Emily came back into the utility room with the hot water bottle wrapped in a fleece blanket, which Bob tucked it into the whelping box beside Willow.

Emily crouched beside Neil. "Do you think she'll be all right?"

"No reason why not," Bob replied. "But with a first litter it's always good to be careful. Ready?" he said suddenly. "Here we go!"

Willow panted and pushed. A tiny shape appeared from her hindquarters, wrapped in what looked like a bag. Neil knew this was the birth sac, which protected the puppy as it grew inside its mother.

"Willow, you've done it!" Emily breathed. "Your very first pup."

The newborn pup was still connected to Willow by the cord that had fed it inside her womb. As if someone had taught her what to do, Willow twisted around so she could reach the cord and bit through it. Then she licked the pup vigorously to get rid of the birth sac.

The pup let out a faint whimpering sound, as if it was protesting.

Bob was grinning. "It's a girl," he announced and added, "It must be a shock, coming out into the big, wide world. It's OK, little one. We'll look after you." He had a towel in his hand, ready to clean up the pup's eyes and mouth, but Willow was doing the job efficiently by herself.

After a minute or two the pup wriggled close to her mom, fastened onto one of her teats, and began to suck.

"Awesome!" Neil said quietly. "Totally awesome!"

Willow nosed the little pup affectionately, and Emily reached out to stroke her damp, white fur with one finger. "She's so tiny!" she said. "Dad, how many pups will Willow have? Dotty had eight!"

"Not as many as that," Bob said. "As a rough guide, the bigger the dog, the bigger the litter. Willow should —"

He broke off as Willow began to pant hard again and he lifted the first pup away from her mom and onto the hot water bottle. The puppy protested with a tiny squeak.

"Sorry, midget," Bob said. "I'll put you back in a minute. Willow might hurt her by mistake while the next one's coming out," he explained to Neil and Emily.

As he spoke, a second puppy appeared from Willow's hindquarters. Bob checked it quickly. "This one's a boy," he said.

Willow cleaned him up like the first one and gently nudged him to start nursing. Bob replaced the first pup and soon the two little bundles of white fluff were sucking happily side by side.

Once the second puppy was feeding, Willow seemed to settle down for a rest. She dropped her nose onto her paws, closed her eyes, and let out a deep sigh.

"Do you think she's finished?" Neil asked. "After just two pups?"

"Maybe," said Bob. "But it's not unusual to have a

long gap between pups. I'll stay and keep an eye on her, but you two go to bed if you like."

"And miss some more pups being born?" Neil said. "No way!"

For a while it looked as if nothing else was happening. Emily went into the kitchen to make some hot chocolate and Carole came down from putting Sarah to bed.

Emily was passing around the hot drinks when Neil noticed that Willow had started to shift uncomfortably. "I think she's started again," he said.

Bob moved the two pups onto the hot water bottle to give Willow more room. For a long time Willow panted and strained, but a puppy didn't appear.

"What's the matter with her?" Neil asked anxiously.

"Probably nothing," Bob said reassuringly, though Neil noticed he was starting to look worried. "The birth can take longer as the mother gets more tired. Or it might mean that the pup is in an awkward position in the birth canal, so it's harder for the mother to push it out."

"Should we call Mike?" Neil suggested.

"Not yet," said Bob. "Let's give Willow a little longer first."

Emily crouched down beside Willow and stroked her head gently. "Kate will never forgive us if anything goes wrong," she said.

Neil thought Willow was starting to look exhausted. It was hard work bringing puppies into the world.

Neil was just beginning to fidget, wanting to go and call Mike Turner, when suddenly Emily exclaimed, "Look! The puppy's coming!"

Relief washed over Neil as he saw another tiny puppy starting to emerge.

"Breech birth," said Bob, sounding serious. "That means the legs are coming first instead of the head. No wonder it was stuck!"

"It's awfully small," Emily said.

Neil could see she was right. This pup was a lot smaller than the two that were now cuddled against the hot water bottle. He started to get anxious again, especially when the pup lay motionless as Willow bit through the cord and licked away the birth sac.

"Is it alive?" Emily asked, her voice tight.

"Can't tell yet," Bob said calmly. "Neil, hand me that towel."

Neil passed it over. Bob used it to pick up the little pup, which lay limply in his hands. Very gently, he cleaned its eyes and mouth, and gave it a rub with the towel.

"It's dead!" Emily exclaimed.

"Call Mike," said Bob, not taking his eyes off the pup.

Emily scrambled to her feet and went out to find Carole. Neil watched his dad, wishing there was something he could do. Willow let out a little whimper, as if she couldn't understand why this pup didn't behave like the others.

Bob climbed carefully to his feet. He held the tiny body between both hands and raised it high in the air.

Neil stared. He had no idea what his dad was doing.

Then Bob swung the pup vigorously toward the floor. "This can help clear fluid from the lungs," he explained.

The puppy didn't move. Bob tried the swing again and again.

Emily came back and watched wide-eyed, tears trickling down her face. "Mike's coming," she said. She was holding Carole's hand tightly.

Bob swung the pup a fourth time and at last Neil saw the tiny body twitch. "It's alive!" he said. He felt like jumping up and down and cheering, but he didn't want to startle Willow, who was watching Bob anxiously.

Bob used the towel to clear the pup's mouth again and gave it another gentle rub. It was wriggling feebly now, and it let out a faint mewing noise.

"There we are," said Bob. "Another girl. Come on, little one, have some milk from your mom."

He put the third pup down in the whelping box, by Willow's side. But the puppy didn't start to feed; she just lay there. Willow tried to nudge her into nursing, but the tiny creature didn't respond.

"She's very weak," said Bob. "That long labor must have tired her out."

"But she'll die if she doesn't nurse!" Emily cried.

"If she can't feed herself, we'll have to feed her," said Carole. "It'll be all right, Emily. It's not the first time. Remember those pups Toby Sparrow brought us? You managed wonderfully with them." She smiled encouragingly at Emily. "I think I've got some of the right milk formula," she added. "I'll go and look."

Bob put the other two pups back with their mom and they both started to suck. He tried again to get the third pup to feed, but with no more success.

Neil kept his eyes fixed on the tiny scrap of white fluff as they waited for Mike Turner to arrive. It felt like forever. The pup didn't move again. Neil could see she was breathing, but he expected every feeble breath to be the last.

He realized he was digging his nails into the palms of his hands. *She won't die!* he vowed to himself.

"Come on," Bob said, trying to sound encouraging. "We've got three pups here. What are we going to call them?"

"Kate might not like our names," Emily pointed out, sniffing and scrubbing her eyes with the back of her hand.

"Then she can change them," said Bob. "The pups will be too small to learn their names for a long time yet."

"Christmas names, then," said Emily, trying to smile. "Because they're born on Christmas morning. What do you think, Neil?"

"Sounds good to me," said Neil. "What about Angel?" He stroked the first pup very gently.

"With a name like that, she'd better be a *really* good dog!" Bob said, grinning.

"And this one can be Tinsel," Emily said, pointing to the second pup. "And the little one . . ."

Her voice faltered and Neil could tell she was thinking that the third pup might not need a name at all.

"The little one is Star," Neil said, speaking louder than he'd meant to. "She's having a tough time, but she'll get over it. She'll be a real star!"

Emily managed a watery smile. "OK, Star it is!"

At last Neil heard the back door open and his mom reappeared, followed by Mike Turner. The vet put his bag down and kneeled beside the whelping box. Bob explained to him what had happened.

Mike nodded, picked Star up, and examined her gently. "There's nothing obviously wrong," he said. "Sometimes you get a weak pup, and the difficult birth doesn't help." He paused, then added, "Caring for her will be quite a job, you know."

"We can do it," Neil said determinedly. "Just tell us what she needs."

"Warmth is most important," Mike said. "Hypothermia is one of the most common causes of death in new pups. This room feels fine and I see you've got the infrared lamp, but you should check the temperature. It should be kept at 79 degrees Fahrenheit."

"I'll get a thermometer," Carole said. "And we can bring in another heater if we need to."

"Fine," said Mike. "The next thing is, you need to keep an eye on Willow. Mothers have been known to reject their pups by pushing them out of the whelping box and letting them die."

"Willow wouldn't do that!" Emily exclaimed, sounding shocked.

"Even the best mother dogs have been known to harm their pups if they're disturbed after the birth. So it's important to keep Willow quiet and happy."

"No problem!" said Neil. He knew that Mike was trying to make them realize how difficult it was going to be to look after Star, but there was no way Neil was going to let Willow's puppy down.

"And then there's feeding, of course," Mike went on. "The pup will need to be fed every two hours until she can suck from Willow herself. Once she can do that, you're home free."

"More sleepless nights!" Carole said.

"I can do it," Neil said. "I don't mind getting up."

"And me," said Emily.

"You'll need a special milk formula," Mike said. "I can go down to the clinic and get —"

"No need," Carole interrupted, showing him the packet she was carrying. "I always keep some of this on hand. It's useful if any of the young boarding dogs are off their food."

"That's fine," said Mike. "Have you got a small feeding bottle or a syringe?"

Carole nodded.

"I'm going to fetch some blankets," Neil said. "I'll make up a bed on the living room sofa and then I'll be able to get up and feed Star."

"I want to do it as well," Emily said. "Mom, can we bring down the folding bed?"

"Yes, I'll help you," Carole said. "Just as soon as Mike has finished."

"Santa Claus won't come if you're not in bed and asleep," Bob said teasingly.

Neil laughed. In the drama of the last hour he'd forgotten all about Christmas presents. "I'm sure he'll time his visit for when we're not feeding Star," he said.

Neil woke in the dark with the loud ring of his alarm clock in his ear. For a second he couldn't figure out where he was. The room was dark, so it wasn't morning, and he felt too tired to have slept through the night.

Then he remembered. He had promised to get up every two hours and feed Star. Before Mike Turner left, he had examined the other two pups and Willow herself. Thankfully, they were all healthy, and Willow hadn't had any more pups to come.

Neil pushed back his blankets and sat up. He was on the living room sofa, and as his eyes got used to the faint light filtering in from the hall he could see Emily curled up on the folding bed beside him. The heavy weight across his feet was Jake.

Yawning, Neil crawled out of his blankets and gave Emily a shake. Then he dragged himself into the kitchen with Jake at his heels.

Carole had left the milk formula on the kitchen table, along with a measuring cup and tiny feeding bottle. Mike Turner had written down the amount Star was to have and Carole had given her the first feed before he left. Neil and Emily had watched carefully so they knew what to do.

As Neil put on the kettle and started to measure out the formula, Emily came in and went straight through to the utility room to check on Willow and the pups.

"They're fine," she told Neil. "Star's still alive."

Until then, Neil hadn't admitted to himself that she might not be. He didn't let Emily see how relieved he felt. "She's gong to stay that way," he said firmly.

When the formula was ready, he took the feeding bottle into the utility room. Starlight was shining softly through the window. Willow and her pups were curled up together in the whelping box, all asleep. Bob and Carole had cleaned them up and given them fresh bedding when the birth was over.

"They're so sweet!" Emily murmured.

Carefully, Neil picked Star out of the huddle of puppies and cradled her on his lap. She was so tiny — a ball of white fluff small enough to nest in his hand, her eyes still tightly closed. Her fur was damp and frizzy where Willow had been cleaning her. She whimpered softly. Emily held the feeding bottle against Star's tiny lips, but at first she turned her head away.

"Remember what Mom did?" Neil said.

Emily nodded, and squeezed out a few drops of milk onto her fingers. She held them for Star to sniff and the pup put out a tiny pink tongue and licked at the milk. Emily offered her the bottle again and this time Star began to suck.

Neil felt a huge smile spreading over his face. "All right!"

The whole house was quiet. Neil felt sleepy, but he wouldn't have missed this for the world. He gazed down at the little white bundle on his lap and willed Star to keep drinking and make herself strong and healthy.

Star didn't finish the whole bottle before her head dropped and she went back to sleep. Emily took her from Neil, cuddled her for a moment, and then put her carefully back into the whelping box with her mom.

Quietly, Neil and Emily went back to the living room. Neil set the alarm clock again; there would be one more feed before the rest of the house got up.

"Star's going to be OK!" Emily said with a blissful smile on her face as she climbed back into bed.

"Maybe," said Neil. He still couldn't help feeling worried. "Somehow, we've got to get her to start feeding from her mom." He frowned into the darkness. Little Star was clearly a fighter, but would that be enough?

CHAPTER EIGHT

Neil awoke to the sound of footsteps going down the hall and a door opening and closing. Beside him on the folding bed, Emily rolled over and sat up.

They had woken up once more in the night to give Star another feed. Now Neil didn't know what time it was, but his stomach told him that breakfast was long overdue. A bulging Christmas stocking lay on the sofa at his feet, and there was another beside Emily's bed. "Hey!" he said. "Santa Claus came after all!"

Before he opened his presents, Neil wanted to check on Star. In the hall, Bob was hanging up the phone. He had a wide grin on his face.

"Merry Christmas, Dad!" Neil said.

"Merry Christmas, Neil. I was just talking to Glen."

"Did you tell him about the puppies?" Emily asked, emerging from the sitting room. She was yawning and rubbing sleep out of her eyes.

Bob's eyes twinkled. "Let's go and find your mom first," he said, leading the way to the kitchen.

As Neil opened the door, a delicious aroma of roasting turkey wafted out. It made him feel hungrier than ever.

Sarah was sitting at the table, wearing her angel costume again and eating toast, while Carole was peeling carrots. Jake was asleep in his basket.

"Have we missed breakfast?" Neil asked, dismayed.

"No, I kept yours hot," Carole said. "We thought we'd let you sleep for a while. You did a wonderful job last night."

"Is Star OK?" Neil said.

"They're all fine," Carole replied. "I gave Star another feed when I got up, and now they're all asleep."

Neil glanced in through the utility room door and saw Willow curled up peacefully with her pups. "Can she feed from Willow yet?" he asked.

Carole shook her head. "No, not yet, but I'm sure it's only a matter of time."

Neil wished he felt as confident as his mom. He sat at the kitchen table and helped himself to cereal.

"What did you say to Glen, Dad?" Emily asked. "Did you tell him about the pups?"

"Yes, and he's thrilled," said Bob. "But he's even more thrilled about something else."

Carole looked up sharply from the carrots. "Kate?"

Bob nodded. "Kate had her baby this morning. A little boy. A few days earlier than expected, but they're both fine."

"Cool!" Neil said through a mouthful of cereal. Emily grinned happily.

"I want to see the new baby," Sarah said. "Can we go now?"

"We'll all go to see him," said Carole, "but not today. Kate will be very tired."

"Glen asked me if we'd keep the pups here for a few days," Bob went on. "Just until Kate comes home from the hospital. Of course I said we would. In any case, it's not a good idea to move Star just yet."

"I hope three puppies *and* a baby won't be too much for Kate," Neil said. "Especially when Star needs so much care."

"I'm sure Kate will be happier if Willow's with her," his dad assured him. "I know she's missed her a lot. But we'll have to wait until Star is stronger before they can go home."

"What did Glen say about Star?" Emily asked.

"He was worried, of course. I said I'd leave it to him how much to tell Kate. And we'll keep him up to date with how she's doing."

Carole brought plates of egg and bacon to the table and set them down in front of Neil and Emily. "You two need a shower to wake you up," she said. "It's Christmas Day and there's a lot to do. How about taking some of the boarding dogs for a walk?"

"Yes!" said Neil. He hesitated, then asked his dad, "Do you think we could take Brutus?"

"Well . . ." Bob stroked his beard. "Maybe if I come with you. He seemed OK first thing when I fed him."

"Great!" Neil attacked his eggs and bacon. "Then we can all see how well he's doing."

The young Doberman leaped to his feet as Neil went into the rescue center. He pushed his nose against the mesh to say hello.

"Hi, Brutus," Neil said, slipping him a dog treat. "How about a walk?"

He was disappointed to see that Brutus backed off again as Bob came in, but at least he didn't growl.

"He's starting to get used to you," Neil said.

Bob opened the door and Neil went in to clip a leash onto Brutus's collar. Then he led Brutus outside.

Snow still lay thickly on the ground. The sky was blue and the sun was shining; it was a perfect day for a walk.

Emily appeared from Kennel Block One with two of the boarding dogs on leashes: a Labrador called Cass, who was a frequent visitor to King Street, and another old friend, a huge mongrel called Bundle. Bob had suggested taking them for a walk with Brutus because they were both reliably good-natured.

As Neil led Brutus across the yard, the Doberman pulled away, as if he was unhappy about being so close to strange dogs. Neil gave him a reassuring pat. "It's OK, boy," he said. "These are friends."

He called to Jake, who was waiting on the back step, and the Border collie bounded down the garden path to the gate that led to the exercise field. His tail waved wildly and he let out a joyful bark.

"There," Neil said as he opened the gate. "Go and run the itch out of your feet."

Jake dashed off, snow scattering under his paws as he ran across the field. Brutus pulled on his leash, whining softly, as if he wanted to go after him. *Well!* Neil thought. *He's not scared of Jake!*

"Should I let him off the leash?" Neil asked.

"OK," said Bob. "But keep a close eye on them."

Neil unclipped the leash and at once Brutus took off after Jake. He leaped up at the Border collie and the two dogs rolled over together in the snow. For a second Neil was anxious, but then he saw that they were just playing, making the most of the snow and the fresh air.

He pulled a ball out of his pocket and threw it. Jake and Brutus raced after it. Jake got there first and, to Neil's relief, Brutus didn't try to fight him for it. He just trotted at Jake's side as Jake brought the ball back to Neil.

"Way to go, boys!" Neil said as they came up, slipping them tidbits from the supply in his pocket.

Then Bob held out a tidbit to Brutus. For a moment it looked as though the big dog would refuse it, but Bob spoke to him in a gentle, soothing voice. Slowly, Brutus moved toward Bob's outstretched hand and took the tidbit. Bob smiled, and so did Neil.

Emily brought Bundle and Cass up for their share and let them off their leashes, too. Bundle joined in the game with the ball, but Cass was too dignified — or, as Emily said, too lazy!

Neil stood watching the three dogs hurtle across the field. He enjoyed the sight of Brutus's strong, well-muscled body and his shining coat. "Just look at him!" he said proudly. "That's not the same dog we found by the garbage cans. He's learning how to play and share with other dogs. He deserves a really good home!"

"As soon as Christmas is over," Emily said, "we'll get Jake Fielding to put something in the paper."

"Yeah," said Neil. He tried to forget about his disappointment that the Meadows family didn't feel able to take the Doberman. "Somewhere there must be somebody who'll realize what a great dog Brutus is!"

Christmas dinner at King Street was as good as it could be. Neil thought his mom had cooked the best turkey in the world and that his dad's chestnut stuffing was unbeatable!

When the meal was over, everyone went into the living room to open their presents. Neil got a dog encyclopedia on CD-ROM and Emily got a new Polaroid camera. Sarah's main present was a big box of paints and some animal stencils. Neil had bought special dog treats for Jake and Willow, and even Fudge had a new plastic house for his cage.

Emily's eyes shone as she examined her new camera. "I'm going to take pictures of Willow and the pups," she said. "To show Kate, when we go and visit her."

"Good idea," said Carole.

"I think Kate's gotten the best Christmas presents of anyone," Emily said. "Three puppies and a baby — you can't get much more special than that!"

* * *

When the last scrap of Christmas wrapping paper had been cleared away, Bob went out to continue with the kennel work. Even on Christmas Day, the dogs had to be cared for, and there was even more to do without Kate and Bev to help.

"We'll come and help, Dad," Emily said. "We'll check on the rescue center first."

"Remember, you're not to go into Brutus's pen," Carole reminded Neil and Emily as they put on warm coats and boots. "I know he's improving, but we still can't be sure he's safe."

Privately, Neil thought Brutus would be fine, but he knew better than to argue.

"And I don't know where Sarah's gone off to," Carole went on. "If she's out there, make sure she's wrapped up well."

"We'll let her cuddle up to a nice, warm dog," Neil promised. "Squirt will love that!"

The sun was already starting to go down when Neil and Emily went out. The snow in the courtyard was freezing again and icicles hung from the gutters.

There was no sign of Sarah until Neil opened the door of the rescue center and heard muffled giggling from his sister. To his amazement, he saw that the door to Brutus's pen was open.

"Squirt!" he exclaimed. "You're not supposed to —"

He stopped, his mouth open in astonishment as he

looked inside the pen. Sarah was kneeling down beside Brutus, and she had draped tinsel around his neck and over his head. She was fixing a paper streamer to his collar like a pair of reins.

Brutus just stood still and looked at her. Neil thought he might even be enjoying the attention. His jaws were wide and his tongue was lolling out as if he was laughing.

"Just look at that!" he said to Emily.

Sarah looked up. "Brutus is a reindeer," she announced. "He's got long legs so he can go really fast. Next year he's going to pull Santa's sleigh."

"Sure, Squirt," Neil said, raising his eyebrows at Emily. "I bet he'll really enjoy that!"

"Neil," Emily said excitedly, "go and get the digital camera. This would make a really good picture for the web site!"

Neil grinned. "You're right, it would."

He dashed back to the house and grabbed the digital camera. By the time he got back to the rescue center, Emily had helped Sarah to take off the coat she was wearing over her angel costume and made her a halo out of tinsel. Sarah posed with one arm around Brutus's neck and a huge smile on her face. Brutus's eyes shone and he was obviously enjoying himself just as much as Sarah.

"That's perfect!" Neil said. "You know, that dog has a real sense of humor. He's just never had the chance to show it."

He took several pictures and the whole time Brutus behaved like the friendliest family dog imaginable. When the photo shoot was finished, he came nosing up to Neil, sniffing at his pocket.

"I know what you want," Neil said, fishing out a dog treat. "There — and you deserve it!"

He took the camera straight into the office to put the picture on the web site, and Emily went with him, leaving Sarah to take the decorations off Brutus and close up the pen.

"We'll make it the home page picture," Emily said excitedly, "and put 'A Merry Christmas from all at

King Street.' It'll show everyone what a great pet Brutus could be."

Neil switched on the computer and uploaded the photos from the digital camera. "I wouldn't let Squirt hear me say this, but she looks really cute!" he said.

He had just started writing a caption when he was interrupted by noises from the kitchen. He heard his mother's voice, high in alarm, and then Sarah's, followed by a deep bark.

Neil jumped to his feet. "That's Brutus. Squirt must have brought him into the house!"

CHAPTER NINE

Neil dashed for the kitchen, with Emily right behind him. It was a rule at King Street that none of the boarding or rescue dogs came into the house. Neil didn't mind the rule being broken, but he guessed his mom would be annoyed, especially if she thought Brutus might be unpredictable.

When he got to the kitchen, Neil saw Brutus standing in the doorway of the utility room, wearing his tinsel reindeer outfit. Sarah was beaming happily, but Carole didn't look so pleased. She had a hand on Jake's collar, restraining him from going over to say hello to the Doberman.

"Neil, thank goodness," Carole said as he came in. "Take Brutus back to his pen, would you? He shouldn't be in here, he'll disturb Willow."

Sarah's grin vanished. "He likes it here," she objected.

"That's not the point," said Carole. "Willow needs to be kept quiet, and besides, you know the rule. If we start breaking it, we'll be up to our ears in dogs in here."

"Sounds good to me," said Neil. Before Carole could speak, he added hurriedly, "OK, Mom, I'm coming."

Slowly and calmly, so as not to alarm Brutus, he crossed the kitchen. He knew he had to get the Doberman out of there before he upset Willow, or did anything to harm her litter. Although Brutus was improving all the time, Neil still couldn't be sure that he could be trusted around such tiny pups.

But Brutus showed no sign of being nervous or aggressive. He looked up at Neil with his fine, intelligent eyes and gave a woof, as if he was saying hello.

"Hi, Brutus," Neil said as he reached the dog and gave him a pat.

Inside the utility room, Willow was sitting up in the whelping box, as if she wasn't sure about the intruder. Neil knew how important it was that she not be disturbed, especially when Star was so weak. He remembered Mike Turner's warning that mother dogs sometimes attacked their own pups if they were upset. "Stay calm, Willow," he said softly.

While Neil stayed beside the Doberman, one hand on the dog's glossy back, Emily went over to Willow and stroked her rough white fur until she settled down again. All the pups were curled up, asleep, and Emily checked to make sure that Star was still breathing. "That's it, girl," she said to Willow as she lay protectively beside the pups. "You take good care of them, you hear?"

While Emily was soothing Willow, Brutus stood motionless in the doorway, looking on with interest. *He couldn't have behaved better*, Neil thought, and he was clearly not upsetting the other dogs at all.

Then, as Emily was getting up from the whelping box, Neil heard the kitchen door fly open. His dad's voice shouted, "Brutus isn't in his pen!"

Neil's stomach lurched. This loud interruption was the last thing Brutus needed, especially from Bob, who hadn't been the Doberman's favorite person from the start.

Neil grabbed Brutus's collar, but the Doberman hardly reacted at all, just swinging his head around to see who the newcomer was.

"Good job, boy!" Neil said, patting him. Brutus seemed quite relaxed, not trembling or showing aggression.

"Well!" Bob said. He had halted just inside the back door, and he wasn't looking too thrilled. "Was this your idea, Neil?"

"No, it was Sarah," Carole said. "She doesn't understand that Brutus is too high-strung to —"

"Brutus is fine, Mom," Neil protested. "You can see he is."

"He wanted to see the little puppies," said Sarah, looking upset.

"All right, crisis over," said Bob. "I thought we'd lost him. Come on, boy, let's put you back where you belong."

"Dad," said Neil, as Bob came over to take the dog, "can't Brutus stay here? Just for now?"

"Now, look, Neil —" Carole began.

"Please!" said Emily. "Brutus has never lived with a real family. He's never had any fun. And it is Christmas."

"He needs to learn how to be a family dog," Neil added.

Carole was trying to look stern, but her mouth was twitching at the corners. Neil felt hopeful. After all, Brutus hardly looked threatening when he was wearing a pair of tinsel antlers!

"It wouldn't do any harm, just for one evening," Bob said.

"Well, all right," Carole said. Neil let out a cheer and Jake gave an approving bark. "But don't think you can make a habit of it," his mom added. "And keep Brutus well out of the way while you're feeding Star."

"Sure, Mom," said Neil.

Neil took off Brutus's decorations, and then he and

Emily took him into the office while they finished updating the web site. The big dog sat quietly beside them, his ears pricked.

"Do you like your picture, Brutus?" Emily asked.

The Doberman gave the computer screen a long look and then let out a bark.

"Is that a yes or a no?" asked Neil.

"It must be a yes," said Emily. "That's the best home page picture we've ever had!"

Neil switched off the computer and led the way into the living room, where Sarah and Bob were watching *The Wizard of Oz*. Brutus padded after

Neil and Emily and flopped down at Bob's feet as if he had been living with them all his life.

When the film ended, Carole called Neil and Emily into the kitchen to give Star her evening feed. They left Brutus snoozing with Jake in front of the living room fire.

While Carole fed Willow in the utility room, Neil brought Star into the kitchen and cuddled her on his lap. He loved the feel of her soft white fur, all fluffed up from Willow's tongue. He was trying hard to convince himself that the tiny pup was growing stronger, but when he compared Star to her brother and sister he had to admit there was a long way to go.

Emily held the feeding bottle and both she and Neil watched anxiously as Star weakly sucked the milk.

"Do you want to do the night feeds again?" Bob asked, turning from the sink where he was washing dishes. "I'll take over if you want."

"No, we can manage, Dad," Neil said. "I want to —"

He broke off as the kitchen door swung open. Brutus appeared in the doorway, and before anyone could make a move he trotted across the kitchen and pushed his nose into Neil's lap, where Star lay.

Neil couldn't help feeling a jolt of alarm. Brutus's head was bigger than the whole of Star's body and he had a lot of teeth. He could swallow the tiny pup in one gulp if he wanted to!

"Brutus!" Emily gasped.

Then Neil saw that they had all been wrong not to trust Brutus, even for a moment. The big dog nosed Star affectionately and his tongue rasped along her coat.

As Star felt the gentle licking she gave a wriggle and let out a tiny squeak. Neil had never seen her respond like that before.

"Hey!" He grinned broadly, feeling a surge of hope for the tiny pup. "It's as if Brutus knows that Star is feeling weak!"

Bob came over to have a look. "You've done a good job with Brutus," he said approvingly. "He's settled down into a wonderful dog. The family who gets him will be very lucky."

Neil glowed inside. It looked like Brutus was having a merry Christmas after all.

After lunch the next day, the Parkers got ready to visit Kate in the hospital. Brutus had been put back into his pen, but Neil had taken him out for a run in the exercise field with Jake that morning.

"Mom," Sarah said excitedly, "I want to take Willow and the puppies to show Kate. Can we?"

Carole was packing up some magazines for Kate and a soft stuffed dog for the new baby. "I'm afraid not," she said gently. "The nurses would never let them into the hospital."

Sarah's mouth dropped. "But Kate will *want* to see them."

"Don't worry," said Emily. She waved an envelope and tucked it into the pocket of her coat. "I took lots of photographs with my new camera. Especially so Kate can see Willow and the pups."

"And Brutus!" said Neil.

In the hospital, Kate was sitting by the side of her bed, wearing a pretty quilted dressing gown. Glen was there, too, grinning from ear to ear as the Parkers peered into the cradle beside the bed.

"Oh, he's *gorgeous*!" exclaimed Carole. "What have you named him?"

"Noel," said Kate. "Because he was born on Christmas Day."

The baby looked very small and crumpled. He was wrapped up in a white blanket and his eyes were tightly closed.

"Look, Kate," said Emily, pulling out the envelope full of photographs. "I took these for you."

Kate laid out the pictures on her bed, exclaiming over Willow and the pups.

"We called that one Angel," Neil told her, pointing to the biggest pup. "And that one is Tinsel."

"And the little one is Star," Emily added. "But if you don't like those names you can change them."

"I wouldn't dream of it," said Kate. "They're perfect names for Christmas pups. Thank you! All of you — for looking after them all so well. I don't know what I would have done without you."

"All part of the Puppy Patrol service," said Bob, smiling.

"Isn't Star small?" Sarah said, examining one of the pictures. "She's the littlest puppy I've ever seen."

"How is she?" Kate asked anxiously. Glen had obviously told her that Star was very weak.

"I'm sure she'll be fine," Carole reassured her. "Neil and Emily have been feeding her every two hours and she's holding her own."

Kate smiled, trying to look brave, but Neil could

see she was still worried. Kate knew just as much about dogs as they did; she would understand that Star wouldn't be out of danger until she could feed from her mom.

"You should have seen Brutus!" he said, hoping to distract Kate. "He really loves Star."

Kate picked up one of the pictures that showed the young Doberman. In the photograph, Brutus was sitting beside Neil, looking down protectively at Star as she lay in Neil's lap.

"He's a fabulous dog," said Glen. His voice was full of admiration.

"He certainly is," Bob agreed. "Little Star has a friend for life."

"Have you managed to find a home for Brutus yet?" Glen asked.

Neil shook his head. "We're going to make a big effort as soon as the holiday is over. We might get Jake Fielding to do an article about him in the *Compton News*."

"Don't worry, somebody will want him," Glen said, fingering the picture thoughtfully. "In fact, you know, we —"

"Glen Paget!" Kate interrupted, laughing. "I know what you're thinking. We just haven't got the space for a new baby, Willow and her pups, *and* a big dog like Brutus."

"I suppose you're right." Glen put the picture down regretfully.

Neil felt a rush of disappointment, although he couldn't help agreeing. He thought the Pagets would be great owners for Brutus, but he knew Kate would have enough to cope with already when she went home. *But somewhere,* Neil thought, *there's a family waiting to give a great home to Brutus. All I have to do is find them!*

CHAPTER TEN

As Bob turned the King Street Kennels' Range Rover into the driveway, Neil saw an unfamiliar car parked there.

"Who can that be?" Carole asked. "I told everybody we were closed Christmas week."

The Range Rover had hardly come to a stop when the door of the car burst open and Jackie Meadows scrambled out.

"Neil! Neil!" She dashed over to him as he got out of the Range Rover. "We've come for Brutus!"

Neil was so dazed for a moment that he could hardly take in what she was telling him.

Jackie grabbed his shoulders and gave him a shake. "Brutus!" she repeated. "He is still here, isn't he? Nobody's come to take him?"

Neil suddenly grasped what Jackie was saying. He felt a big bubble of happiness expanding inside him. "No," he managed to say. "He's still here."

"He's waiting for you," Emily said. She was grinning widely. "He's been your dog all along."

Mr. and Mrs. Meadows followed Jackie across the yard and shook hands with Bob and Carole. "We really didn't feel we could risk Brutus with our twins at first," Mr. Meadows said. "They can be pretty lively and they might startle Brutus without meaning to."

"And then we saw the picture on your web site," Mrs. Meadows continued. "That lovely photograph of Brutus with your little girl. It's clear he's good with children. So we talked it over and —"

"And we decided to adopt him!" Jackie finished. Anxiously, she added, "We can adopt him, can't we?"

"I can't think of anyone better," Carole told her, smiling, while Neil said, "You bet!"

"I'm sorry to disturb you today," Mrs. Meadows went on, "but Jackie insisted on coming over right away. My mom and dad are at home with Ben and Nicky. I didn't want to overwhelm Brutus!"

"Can we take him now?" Jackie asked eagerly.

"Of course you can," said Carole. "Bob, if you take them over to the rescue center, I'll go into the office and sort out the paperwork."

She let herself into the house while the rest of the Parkers led the Meadows family through the side gate and into the rescue center.

Brutus leaped up as soon as he saw Jackie and padded up to the front of the pen. Neil opened the door for her. She went in, kneeled down, and flung her arms around Brutus.

"You're ours!" she said. "You're really ours!"

Her parents stood looking down at them, smiling, while Brutus licked her face enthusiastically. His stumpy tail was wagging vigorously. Neil and Emily exchanged a satisfied nod. There was nothing they liked better than matching up a dog with an owner who would give it the best possible home.

"I have to say that you're getting a wonderful dog," Bob told Mr. and Mrs. Meadows. "A Doberman is one of the bravest and most faithful dogs around."

"Do you hear that, Brutus?" Jackie whispered. She leaned closer to him, as if she was sharing a secret. "I knew you were perfect!"

"I see from the web site that you hold obedience classes," Mr. Meadows said.

"That's right," said Bob. "Sunday mornings and Wednesday evenings."

"Then I think we'd better book Brutus in for a course," said Mr. Meadows. "He's had a bad start, but I'm sure he'll soon learn."

"I'll bring him," Jackie said, looking up with her face glowing. "You'd like that, wouldn't you, boy?"

Brutus gave a loud woof, and planted a paw on her knee.

"I think we can call that a yes," said Neil.

While Mr. and Mrs. Meadows filled out forms with Carole in the office, Neil and Emily took Jackie and Brutus into the kitchen. It was time for Star's next feeding. Neil made up the milk formula while Jackie and Emily went to look at Willow's pups.

When he took the feeding bottle into the utility room, he found Jackie sitting on the floor with Tinsel on her lap. Sarah was cuddling Angel, while Emily gently cradled Star. Brutus nosed his tiny friend and gave her another lick. Willow had left the whelping box to have a drink and say hello to Jake. Neil was relieved to see that she looked quite calm about all the human and doggy visitors.

"Do you really have to feed Star every two hours?" Jackie asked. "In the night as well?"

"In the night as well," Emily confirmed.

"That's right," said Neil. "For as long as she needs us."

After all the excitement, he was just beginning to realize how sleepy he was feeling. He wasn't looking forward to another disturbed night, but he was determined not to share Star's care with anyone but Emily. They had promised Mike that they would be responsible for her, and they would see it through.

Neil held the feeding bottle to Star's lips but, to his dismay, she refused to suck. Even Carole's trick of letting her lick milk from his fingers didn't work this time. Star made tiny mewing noises and scrabbled her paws against Emily's hands, and every time Neil tried to give her the bottle she turned her head away.

"What's the matter with her?" Emily asked desperately. "She was fine earlier on. She can't give up now, she just can't!"

Sarah looked up from petting Angel, her lip quivering.

"She's *got* to eat," Neil said determinedly. He couldn't bear to think that, after all their efforts, Star might not survive. "Come on, midget — drink some milk!"

Very gently he tried to guide Star's head toward the bottle, but she wriggled away before he could get the end into her mouth. Neil let out a frustrated sigh.

"What are you going to do?" Jackie asked.

"Tell Dad," said Emily. She handed Star over to Neil. "I'll go and get him."

Brutus gave Star a tiny lick, as if he felt just as worried as Neil. Neil stroked the little pup's fuzzy white fur and put her back in the whelping box beside Willow, who was just settling down again.

Star gave a wriggle and cuddled up close to her mom. Then, to Neil's utter astonishment, she took one of Willow's teats into her mouth and began to suck.

Neil stared. "She's doing it!" he whispered. "She's feeding properly!"

"Oh, wow!" said Jackie.

"Hooray!" shouted Sarah.

At that moment, Emily came back into the utility room with Bob. Neil waved urgently to warn them to keep still and they both stood in the doorway, watching the tiny pup as she sucked blissfully.

"No wonder she didn't want the bottle," said Neil. "It's a pretty poor substitute for the real thing!"

"Will Star be OK now?" Emily asked Bob.

"I'm sure she will," her dad replied. "That was the big hurdle — to get her feeding from her mom. We'll keep an eye on her, obviously, but I don't think there's anything to worry about anymore."

"And no more getting up in the middle of the night!" Neil said with relief. "You know what?" he added to Jackie. "I think Brutus helped Star to get better, too."

"Really?"

"Really. Brutus seemed to know that Star was weaker than the others, and he paid extra attention to her."

Jackie put her arms around Brutus and gave him a hug. "You're the best, Brutus! I always knew it."

Neil heard the door from the hall opening, and voices in the kitchen. "That's your mom and dad," he said to Jackie. "We'd better go. It's bad for Willow to have too many people in here."

Reluctantly, he tore his eyes away from little Star and led the way into the kitchen. Carole was explaining to Mr. and Mrs. Meadows about the diet instructions she'd given them for Brutus.

"Mom," Neil said, "Star's feeding from Willow!"

Carole's face lit up with relief and happiness. "At last! That's wonderful news."

Jackie was bubbling over with excitement, telling her mom and dad how Neil and Emily had been looking after Star.

"I'm certainly impressed with what I've seen here," said Mr. Meadows, shaking Bob's hand.

"We do our best," said Bob, smiling.

"Little Star probably wouldn't be here without you," said Jackie. "And I wouldn't have Brutus. I think you're all great!"

Neil felt himself starting to turn red. "Oh, well," he said, "that's what we do. If there's a dog in trouble, just send for the Puppy Patrol!"